About the Author

Born in Staffordshire, Christine grew up in an Anglo-Irish family. She attended a Catholic convent and grammar school and attained a BA Hons in Business Studies.

She has a wonderful daughter and two beautiful grandchildren,
Max aged 7 and Kristen aged 2.

Christine Johnson

Max, Mouse and the Doll's House

AUSTIN MACAULEY PUBLISHERS™

LONDON • CAMBRIDGE • NEW YORK • SHARJAH

A CIP catalogue record for this title is available from the British Library.

ISBN 9781787106659 (Paperback)
ISBN 9781787106666 (E-Book)

www.austinmacauley.com

First Published (2018)
Austin Macauley Publishers™ Ltd.
25 Canada Square
Canary Wharf
London
E14 5LQ

Dedication

For my daughter and her two wonderful children.

Book 1

The Doll's House

Max liked to sleep at Nani's house some Saturday nights when his mum and dad went out with their friends to grown-up places. He usually went with them, but about once a month, Mum and Dad went out to a posh restaurant with their friends, so they could talk about grown-up things without having to watch out for the children. Max didn't mind going to Nani's, he quite liked it really because she played with him and he could have pop and watch cartoons on the TV.

When Max stayed the night at his grandma's, he slept in the room that used to be his mum's room. It was a small room; in fact, his Nani had a small house which was a bit of a funny shape, but what he really liked about the room that he slept in was that in it, there was a doll's house. He and his Nani used to play with the doll's house whenever he visited.

The doll's house comprised of four rooms, two up and two down. There was a sitting room, a dining room complete with wooden furniture and two bedrooms, one single and one double, complete with beds, dressing tables and wardrobes and the beds were dressed with sheets, pillows and eiderdowns. The doll's house had belonged to Max's Nani Christine when she was a little girl and even when she had outgrown the doll's house, she could never bring herself to part with it. Max's Mummy had played with it when she was a little girl and still, the doll's house remained in her bedroom. And so, it was that Max also played with it. Although he thought it was a bit of a girl's toy, he didn't care because he liked playing with it, and he and Nani used to arrange the furniture in all the rooms to make it nice and tidy. The doll's house only had one resident and that was a little Mouse dressed in stripy RED pyjamas. Max would re-arrange the furniture in the house, make up the beds and put Mouse into one of the newly made beds and tuck him up to sleep before he closed the doll's house front door.

This particular Saturday, Max and Nani had been out for the day and he was to stay the night at her house. At about 7 p.m. that night, Max got into his pyjamas and Nani gave him a drink and said that it was time for bed. "Up the wooden hills," she said and they were indeed really steep stairs to climb, and Max and Nani climbed them on all fours until they reached the top and Max ran into the bedroom and jumped into bed. Nani read him quite a few bedtime stories and sang to him until he fell sound asleep. She tucked him up, gave him a goodnight kiss and left the room, leaving the door ajar and the landing light on so that there was a glimmer of light in the room.

A few hours went by before Nani went to bed, turning off all the lights, except for the lamp on the landing and soon she, too, was fast asleep.

Book 2

In the Middle of the Night

In the middle of the night, Max was woken by a banging noise and once he had opened his eyes and pulled himself round from his sleep, he sat up in bed to listen. He couldn't believe what he saw and heard.

Bang, Bang, Bang, "You let me in, let me in, I say. I've got to get into the house." And there on top of the doll's house was a monkey, a little chimpanzee, to be precise, jumping about on the roof of the doll's house and shouting at the top of his voice, "Let me in, I tell you, let me in."

From inside the doll's house, Max heard another voice, "You get down off my roof, you'll break the tiles. Go away and leave me alone."

On hearing all this shouting, Max piped up, "What's going on, what's all the row about?"

The chimpanzee answered, "I need to get into the doll's house and Mouse won't let me in. Anyway, who are you?"

"I'm Max and this is my Nani's doll's house. Why do you want to get into the house?"

Just then, the door of the house opened and Mouse stood in the doorway. "Oh, it's you, Max. Will you tell that monkey to go away," said Mouse.

"How do you know my name?" asked Max.

"Because you play with the doll's house every time you come to stay with your Nani and you tidy my room and tuck me up in bed and very nice of you it is," said Mouse.

"Oh well, there's no need for introductions then," said Max. "Now, Mouse, tell me what's going on."

Mouse went on to explain, "This Charlie chimpanzee monkey has been jumping on my roof for days now, all day, all night, shouting to be let into the house. I asked him why he wanted to come into the house and he came up with some cock and bull story about the door in my cellar leading to his home in the jungle. Apparently, he says he got lost playing hide and seek with his sister and he found himself going through a doorway which led into my cellar and he has to get back through the door to get back to the jungle and find his family. What kind of daft story is that?"

"Is that true?" asked Max.

"Yes, of course it's true, I wouldn't lie about a thing like that," said Charlie and he went on to explain. "I was playing hide and seek with my little sister, Imogen, I was hiding and my sister was the one looking for me. Anyway, I waited and waited for her to find me, but she never came and then I couldn't find my way home. My mum and dad will be worried sick."

Book 3

Thinking and Shrinking

"What are we going to do then?" asked Mouse. "We can't let him go back into the jungle on his own, he might get attacked."

"I agree," said Max. "But how am I going to get into the doll's house and go with you both through the cellar door? I'm too big."

"I know you're too big now," said Mouse, "but if you make yourself small, you will be small enough to go with us."

"How am I going to make myself small?" asked Max. "That's impossible, I can't make myself small."

"Of course you can," responded Mouse. "Now, here's what you have to do. No talking everybody."

Both Max and Charlie the Chimp stood perfectly still and didn't utter a word and it was all quiet in the bedroom.

"Now, Max, close your eyes, close them really tight. Now take a big deep breath in and think yourself small," instructed Mouse and Max did as he was told. He closed his eyes tight shut, took a deep breath in and thought himself small, and sure enough, he felt a funny feeling in his body and he felt as if he was disappearing, and when he opened his eyes, everything around him was bigger than he was. The room appeared massive, his bed was too high for him to climb on to and the doll's house looked like a mansion and when he looked at Mouse and Charlie, he was about as small as them.

"Wow," said Max. "What's happened to me? I'm teeny, tiny. How do I go back to being as big as I was? What if I can't and I stay teeny, tiny forever?"

"Don't worry about that, Max," said Mouse. "You'll think yourself big, just like you thought yourself small and everything will be OK."

"OK," said Max. "If you say so, I do hope so."

"Right," said Mouse. "Now that you are small enough to come into the doll's house, you can come with Charlie and me down to the cellar, through the door and we can take Charlie back to his family in the jungle. Are you in?"

"You bet your life I'm in," said Max and as the front door of the doll's house shut behind them, they made their way through the house, down the stairs into the cellar and stood in front of the door that would lead them into the jungle.

Charlie was so excited that he started jumping up and down, "Come on, come on. Open the door, let's go, hurry!"

"Not so fast," said Max. "We need to think about this, we need a plan. I've never been into the jungle before and neither has Mouse"

"We'll be fine," said Charlie. "I know a few animal friends who will be able to help us find my family."

"And who might they be?" enquired Max. "We need to know who to look for."

"Well," said Charlie, "first of all, we need to find Seb the Snake, Edward the Eagle and Ollie the Elephant. That should do the trick."

On opening the cellar door, a wall of heat hit them. It was like stepping off an aeroplane on arriving at a holiday destination abroad, except that they weren't looking at a concrete jungle, but a lush green tropical land. It was absolutely beautiful, but terrifying at the same time. "Come on," said Charlie, "let's go." Because Charlie was brought up in the jungle, he wasn't afraid, but Max and Mouse stepped out with trepidation.

"Hold on," said Max. "I'm still teeny, tiny. I can't go like this. How am I going to protect Mouse if I'm as small as he is? I need to go back to my original size."

"That's easy," said Mouse, "do what you did before, but instead of thinking yourself small, think yourself big." So Max closed his eyes tight shut, took a deep breath and willed himself big. He felt a funny feeling as if he was bursting out of his clothes and when he opened his eyes and looked down at himself and at Mouse, he realised it had worked and he was as big as he was before.

"Are you ready, Max?" asked Charlie. "Can we go now?"

"Do you know where you're going?" asked Max.

"'Course," said Charlie. "Come on, let's go." And off they set through the green tropical plants, along a narrow track deeper into the jungle.

"Where are we heading?" shouted Max, as Charlie ran ahead in front of them

"What?" shouted Charlie.

"Slow down, Charlie!" shouted Max and Mouse. "Where are we heading? You seem to forget that we're strangers to the jungle and you have to slow down and stay with us."

Charlie stopped in his tracks and waited for Max and Mouse to catch up with him. "OK," said Charlie. "Let's take a break and I'll fill you in with my plan."

"Oh, you have a plan, well, that sounds good," said Max, as he and Mouse caught him up.

They all sat down at the bottom of a great palm tree and waited for Charlie to tell them what his plan was for finding his parents, and as they eagerly awaited Charlie's utterances, they heard a hissing sound coming from one of the branches of the palm tree. They all looked up above into the branches of the tree and, lo and behold, they saw the most enormous snake they had ever seen.

"Ssss Ssss... Hello, Charlie," said the snake. "What are you doing here and who are your friends? I've never seen species such as these in the jungle."

"Oh, hello, Seb," said Charlie. "These are my friends: Max, he's a human being and Mouse, well, he's a mouse, and I got lost in the jungle when I was playing hide and seek with my sister and I went through a door in the jungle

and ended up in Mouse's house which was in Max's Nani's bedroom. It's a long story, but that's the gist of it."

"Wow," said Seb, "that's a ssstrange ssstory. Anyway, my name is Ssseb. How can I help you?" asked Seb as he slid down from the branch of the tree and slithered alongside them.

"Well," said Max, "as you know Charlie got lost and needs to find his parents and his sister and he's not sure where they are or which way to go to find them. Mouse and I agreed to help him. We also need to get back to the doll's house in Nani's bedroom after Charlie finds them."

"Do you know whereabouts you got lossst, Charlie?" asked Seb.

"I have no idea," responded Charlie. "Except that we had been to a Chimpanzees' tea party when I got lost."

"Oh, that's a bit of a problem," said Seb.

"Why?" they all asked.

"Well, the chimpanzees' tea party is held way into the middle of the jungle, not sure where. I do know that the chimpanzees' tea party is held every afternoon and if I ask my friend Ed the eagle, he may be able to fly high above the jungle and see where the tea party is being held. Ed has an eagle eye so he'll be able to spy the exact place. So, what do you say, fellas, shall I call him and ask him to help?" asked Seb.

"Yes, please," said Charlie. "That would be great."

Book 4

Edward the Eagle

Seb slithered away from them and proceeded to slide his way up the trunk of a nearby tree. He disappeared into the lush, green leaves.

"He's gone." said Max. "Where has he gone? He's disappeared."

"Don't worry," said Charlie, "he's just slithering higher into the tree to see if he can see Edward the eagle and get closer so that he can speak with him."

"Oh!" said Max. Max and Mouse both looked up into the tree and waited.

Seb caught sight of Edward perched on the highest branch of the tree and he shouted,

"Ed, Ed, can you hear me? It's Seb. I need your help."

Edward the eagle heard the hissey voice of Seb the snake and shouted back,

"What you do want? I'm busy."

"What do you mean, busy?" Seb shouted. "You don't look busy to me. You're just sitting there on the top branch, doing nothing. Are you going to help me or not?"

"Oh, alright," said Ed. "Wait there, I'll fly down to where you are."

Ed expanded his enormous wings and took off from the highest branch and descended, almost in slow motion, landing near to where Seb was coiled around a branch further down the tree.

"Now, what's up?" said Ed. "What do you want?" Seb explained to him that he had met Charlie and his friends, Max and Mouse, who were helping Charlie find his parents and sister and he wanted Ed to fly

around to see if he could find out where the chimpanzees' tea party was being held.

"Why didn't you say so before," answered Ed. "I can do that, no problem."

"That's really kind of you Ed. Can you do this now?" asked Seb.

"Yep, 'course I can." Ed took to the skies, flying high above the trees and out into the distance across the jungle.

Max, Mouse and Charlie saw the eagle take off from the tree and all stood up looking in awe at the great eagle.

"Wow," said Max, "he's magnificent, he's massive, he's the biggest bird I've ever seen."

"Should I be afraid?" asked Mouse.

"No, you'll be OK," said Max. "Anyway, I'll look after you and he's Seb's friend, so I don't think he's going to eat you."

"Thanks for that," said Mouse. "Now, I'm not really afraid."

Before they knew it, Seb had slithered back down the tree and was curled up beside them sitting at the base of the great palm tree. They waited and waited for Ed to get back to them with some news.

They had been waiting for so long, that Mouse felt sleepy, especially as he was used to spending all his time in bed in Nani's doll's house. Max was a bit tired too. Charlie had stopped jumping around and Seb just lay there hissing and hissing with his long forked tongue slipping in and out of his mouth, making sure that there was nothing dangerous lurking around them.

"Don't worry," said Seb, "I'll keep a lookout if you all want to take a nap."

"Thanks Seb, but no, we're all OK. Aren't we folks?" said Max.

All of a sudden, Ed the eagle appeared out of nowhere and was soaring high above them in the sky. He managed a low circular fly-past and landed gracefully alongside them.

"Have I ever told you that I have an eagle eye, the greatest eagle eye in all of the jungle?" boasted Ed.

"No, but you have now," said Seb. "What news? Have you located the chimpanzees' tea party?"

"I sure have," answered Ed, "it's being held in a clearing, at the other side of Mumble Mountain."

"That's great," said Charlie, who had suddenly started to jump up and down again. "Come on, let's go."

"Hold your water!" shouted Max. "How far is Mumble Mountain and how are we going to get there?"

"You'll need a taxi," said Seb.

"A taxi," retorted Max. "There aren't any taxis in the jungle, don't be daft."

"Not that kind of taxi, Max," said Seb. "I have a friend who runs a taxi service, so to speak, his name is Ollie the elephant and he transports his friends around the jungle, when they are too tired to walk."

"Oh!" said Max. "Do you think he will take us to the other side of Mumble Mountain to the chimpanzees' tea party?"

"Well, I don't see why not. We'd better go and ask him, but there is just one thing."

"What's that?" asked Max.

"Well," said Seb, "Ollie the elephant is a little afraid of mice, so Mouse you'd better get Max to put you in his pocket, we don't want you to frighten him to death."

"I don't mind that," said Mouse. "Max has said that he will look after me."

"Fine by me," agreed Max, as he bent down and picked Mouse up and carefully placed him in his pocket.

"Well," said Ed the eagle, "if I can be of any further help, I'll get off and go about my business."

"Thanks a lot Ed," they all said. "You've been a great help." Ed then expanded his wings and took to the skies. As he soared higher, he shouted,

"Take care, I'll be hovering about as you go on your journey, flying over-high and keeping an eagle eye on you all. Goodbye, bye," and he disappeared into the distance.

"OK folks," said Seb, "come on, Charlie, Max and Mouse in your pocket, let's go and find Ollie. He won't be far away." And they all set off to find the jungle taxi service.

Book 5

Ollie's Taxi Service

Seb led the way, slithering along the path through the jungle at some considerable speed, with Charlie, Max and Mouse – peeping out of Max's pocket – following closely behind. Seb – his tongue continually flicking out of his mouth as he tried to catch scent of the elephants – suddenly stopped. Charlie and Max came to a halt behind him.

"What are you doing?" asked Max.

"I'm just listening," replied Seb.

"Listening to what?" said Max.

"Shush, I'm just listening," he said. The jungle wasn't silent, there were birds squawking and flying overhead, monkeys were chattering loudly and beating their chests. What was he listening for. Then, they all heard it. A loud trumpeting, trumpety, trump, trump, trump. "There he is!" shouted Seb.

"Where?" asked Charlie and Max.

"Over there where the trees are rustling, he's having his dinner."

Max, Charlie and Mouse looked all around and there over to their right, they saw an enormous elephant tugging away at the branches of a tree with his trunk.

"Ollie, Ollie!" shouted Seb. "It's Seb, have you got a minute?" Ollie stopped tugging at the trees and looked around to see Seb, a monkey and a human being.

What do they want? wondered Ollie. Ollie lumbered in their direction and stopped short in front of them. "Oh, hello Seb," said Ollie. "What brings you here?" And Seb proceeded to tell Ollie the story of Charlie and Max, the doll's house and their journey into the jungle to find Charlie's parents and sister. He omitted to mention Mouse in Max's pocket, but it was too late. Mouse let out a loud squeak, squeak, squeak, which Ollie heard and then he saw the mouse.

"Whahh, Whahh!" Ollie trumpeted and at the same time, he appeared to lift off all fours into the air.

"Calm down, Ollie," ordered Seb. "It's only a mouse, what's the problem?"

"I don't like mice," said Ollie. "They frighten me."

"Oh, come on, Ollie, there's nothing to be frightened of, it's a teeny, tiny mouse. How can Mouse hurt you? You are way bigger than he is."

"Well," said Ollie. "I've always been frightened of mice ever since I was little and it was all Ruby mouse's fault. She used to run out in front of me and frighten the wits out of me and ever since, I've been frightened of mice. She doesn't run out in front of me now, now that I am bigger, but I always keep my eye out for her in case she does."

"That's daft, Ollie," said Seb. "Now say hello to Mouse. He's in Max's pocket and he isn't going to run anywhere."

"OK," said Ollie and he proceeded to come closer and put out his trunk to Mouse and Mouse patted it and said:

"Hello, Ollie, I've never seen an elephant before because there aren't any near my home in England, except of course in the zoo and I've never been to the zoo, so you're the first elephant I have ever seen. How do you do?"

"I'm very well, thank you, Mouse, and I'm very pleased to meet you. I don't think I'm frightened of mice anymore," said Ollie. "Anyway, what is it that you want, can I help you in any way?" asked Ollie.

"Well, thank goodness we've gotten that out of the way and we can now all be friends," said Seb, and he then told Ollie that they needed a taxi to take them to the other side of Mumble Mountain to the chimpanzees' tea party to find Charlie's family.

"That'll be no problem," said Ollie. "I can take you myself. I can give you a ride, so hop on."

"What do you mean 'hop on'?" asked Max and Ollie told them all to climb on to his back and he would transport them to the tea party.

"How can we 'hop on'?" asked Max. "We need a ladder to get onto your back."

"No, you don't," replied Ollie. "There are no ladders in the jungle. Come round and stand in front of me," and with that, Max walked around to the front of the elephant, Ollie curled his trunk around Max's waist and swung him up and over onto his back. "Right," ordered Ollie, "Charlie, you're bouncy enough to spring onto my back on your own and Seb, you can curl your body around my tail and we can all get going."

Charlie ran up the nearest tree and swung from a branch to land on the elephant's back behind Max and Seb, as ordered, curled his body around Ollie's tail and then they were off through the jungle in the direction of Mumble Mountain and the chimpanzees' tea party.

Book 6

The Journey over Mumble Mountain

Ollie lumbered off with Charlie and Max on his back, Mouse was in Max's pocket and Seb was clinging onto Ollie's tail. It was a bumpy ride and Max, Charlie and Mouse were riding high, sitting behind Ollie's big ears. The views were fabulous, but they both had to duck under tree branches from time to time to stop getting knocked off Ollie's back. Max and Mouse marvelled at all the sounds of the jungle, birds of every colour of the rainbow squawked and flew overhead, circling the "taxi" and its passengers, monkeys were chattering and looked as if they were flying from branch to branch and appearing to follow them. Charlie chattered away with the jungle monkeys. Max and Mouse didn't know what they were talking about, because they didn't speak "Monkey" but they thought at first that the monkeys were talking about the weather or something, but then it occurred to Max that perhaps they were telling Charlie that they were also going to the chimpanzees' tea party and so, they could show Ollie the way. *Well*, thought Max. *That will be good and they are welcome to come along with us.*

Ollie made his way through the jungle until he came to the base of Mumble Mountain, and Max took one look and wondered how Ollie was ever going to climb to the top and down the other side when Ollie must have read his mind and said, "Don't worry, Max, we'll make it. It's not the first time I've taxied people to the other side. I'm big and strong and I know the easiest path. So hold on to my ears and lean forward as we start to ascend."

"Thanks, Ollie," said Max, feeling a little safer and he clung to Ollie's ears and leaned forward as requested and Ollie proceeded to climb up the winding path on Mumble Mountain. It was a difficult ride for Max, but Charlie didn't seem afraid, he was bouncing up and down with excitement, he nearly fell off a number of times, but he was agile and bendy and managed to stay

aboard. Max kept looking at his pocket to make sure that Mouse was still inside and he was.

As they were nearing the top of Mumble Mountain, they heard a voice shouting to them, "Hey, Hey, stop. Ollie, stop."

"What!" shouted Ollie and there on the ground was a mouse. "Oh, it's you Ruby. What do you want? I'm not frightened of you anymore."

"What do you mean you're not frightened of me anymore? I wasn't aware that you were ever frightened of me. You have always been much bigger than me, even when we were small, so how could you have ever been frightened of a mouse?"

"Well, I was, because you used to run around in front of me, but I'm not now. So what do you want?" asked Ollie.

"I wondered if I could have a lift. I'm on my way to the chimpanzees' tea party for something to eat and I'm getting tired. Anyway, who are your passengers?

I can see Seb clinging to your tail, but who's on your back?" asked Ruby.

"This is Max and he has Mouse in his pocket and that's Charlie and I am taking them to find Charlie's mum, dad and sister, because he got lost and he thinks that he might find them at the tea party," replied Ollie.

"That's Max you say and he has a mouse in his pocket? What kind of mouse? Is he handsome?" asked Ruby and with that, Mouse poked his head out of Max's pocket and looked at Ruby and said:

"Well, helloooo."

"Hello to you, too, Mouse," replied Ruby and she thought him such a handsome mouse, a mouse she would like to get to know better and Mouse, well, he thought Ruby was the prettiest mouse he had ever seen, in her little bright red dress with white polka-dots all over it.

Ollie interrupted the conversation and said, "Come on then Ruby, climb aboard and you'd better hop into Max's other pocket." And with no hesitation, Ruby ran up Ollie's leg and popped herself into the pocket and peeped out again to take another look at Mouse.

As Ollie continued to descend Mumble Mountain, he told his passengers all to hold on tight and lean back this time. As they got half way down the mountain path, they could see a clearing in the distance. The grassy clearing was set out with benches and tables covered in red-checked tablecloths and families of monkeys were coming from every corner, carrying picnic baskets and the little monkeys were carrying bats and balls and skipping ropes. It was an amazing sight, all the monkey families were chattering and laughing and running now to find a table to sit at for the tea party.

Ollie got his passengers safely to the bottom of Mumble Mountain and continued along the path towards the clearing. By this time, there were more monkeys, coming from everywhere, along their path and Charlie was chattering to them all. Soon, they came to the end of the path and into the clearing. Flags were flying, bunting was strung up in the trees and balloons were floating overhead and being burst by the colourful birds circling overhead.

"Are we here, can we get down now?" asked Max.

"You sure can," replied Ollie.

Seb uncurled himself from Ollie's tail and Ollie swung his trunk up and, over his head, curled his trunk around Max's waist and swung him over and down to the ground, Mouse and Ruby still snuggled into his pockets and well, Charlie had already bounced himself off Ollie's back and was still jumping up and down on the grass.

Book 7

The Chimpanzees' Tea Party

Charlie ran out into the tea party amongst all the other monkeys.

"Mum, Dad, Imogen, it's me, Charlie. Are you here?" he shouted at the top of his voice, but there was so much noise talking, shouting and laughing and squealing from the baby monkeys that Charlie couldn't be heard. Ollie, Max, Mouse, Ruby and Seb stood at the entrance to the tea party clearing and Max asked:

"What are we going to do? How can we help Charlie find his family?" They all stood looking at Max and then Max stood tall, took on an air of authority and commanded, "Right. We all go in different directions and ask the monkeys on each table if they have lost their son. OK?" They all nodded in agreement.

"Ollie and Seb, you go over to the left side of the clearing. Mouse and Ruby, you take the middle and I will go over to the right side tables. Are we all in?" asked Max.

"Aye, Aye Captain," they all responded.

They all went off in their different directions to ask all the monkeys on their route whilst Charlie was going haphazardly from table to table, shouting, "Mum, Dad, Imogen. Are you here?"

Ollie lumbered to the left, along with Seb, asking the monkeys on the tables if they had seen Charlie's mum and dad and sister, Imogen, but all said that they had not. In fact, they said that they had not seen Charlie's family for some time, as they'd not been to the chimpanzees' tea party for ages.

Mouse and Ruby ran off through the middle of the tables and asked the same thing, but again, all the chimpanzees said they had not seen Charlie's family at the tea party for some time. Mouse and Ruby then looked at one another and decided it was time for tea, so they ran off to find the table with the most cake and chocolate to nibble at.

Max proceeded to the right hand side of the tea party and walked along the tables, looking to see if any of the chimpanzees looked sad, when he came across a couple of chimpanzees and a little chimpanzee dressed in a lovely pink frock, all looking sad and not speaking or laughing, just eating their tea cakes and bananas and sipping their tea. Max approached them and said, "Excuse me, I know that you don't know me but I wondered why you all looked so sad at such a happy time and I wondered if it was because you had lost your son, Charlie."

The Mum and Dad chimpanzees both stood up and said, "Yes, yes, we have a son called Charlie and he went missing some time ago. He was playing hide and seek with his sister, Imogen, and he got lost. We looked everywhere for him every day and couldn't find him and we are all distraught. Do you know where he is?"

"I certainly do," replied Max, "he's here at the tea party. It's a long story, but my friend Mouse and I and our jungle friends, Ollie, Seb and Ruby have been helping Charlie to find you. So, we must go and find him, because he's frantically looking for you all around the tea party tables."

Charlie's family jumped up from the table and hugged Max. "Thank you, oh, thank you. Let's go please," said Charlie's mum and all proceeded to the centre of the tea party.

When they arrived in the middle of all the hubbub, Max and Charlie's family shouted at the tops of their voices, "Charlie, Charlie, where are you? It's Mum, Dad and Imogen."

Ollie heard all the shouting and saw Max and the chimpanzees in the middle of the tea party clearing. He looked all around and being taller than everyone else, he had a clear view of what was going on all over the party. Then he saw Charlie, jumping around between the tables on the left, and as he was closer to Charlie than anyone else, he ran, yes ran towards Charlie and within a minute, he was standing in front of Charlie.

"Charlie, Charlie!" trumpeted Ollie. "Calm down, calm down, we've found your parents and sister."

Charlie stopped in his tracks. "What?" he said.

"We've found your family," replied Ollie.

"Where? Where? I can't believe it," said Charlie.

"OK, take deep breaths. They're with Max and I can see them. Come with me."

By this time, Seb had caught up with Ollie. "What's going on?" he asked. "I can't see anything from ground level in the grass."

"We've found Charlie's family, Seb, keep up," said Ollie.

"Where?" asked Seb.

"They're over there with Max. Come on, let's go before we lose them again!" shouted Ollie. Ollie trumpeted loudly and managed to get Max's attention. "I'm with Charlie and Seb, I can see you. Are you with Charlie's family? Stand still, we're coming over," and with that, Ollie, Seb and Charlie made their way to the centre of the party where Max and Charlie's family were standing.

Max saw Ollie, Seb and Charlie running towards him and he turned to Charlie's parents and said, "We've found Charlie, he's running towards us with my friends Ollie the elephant and Seb the snake." And there between the tables, they all saw Ollie, Charlie and Seb running towards them. To be fair, Seb was slithering at great speed at their feet and amazingly, he was keeping up with them.

What a reunion when Charlie ran into the arms of his mother, father and sister and they were hugging and kissing and crying and laughing. "We thought we'd lost you for ever," cried Charlie's mum.

"I thought I'd lost you for ever, too. If it wasn't for my new friends Max, Ollie, Seb and Ed, he's an eagle by the way and he spotted where the tea party was being held and Ollie, well he gave us a lift over Mumble Mountain and Max and Seb helped me find you. Oh, and there's also Mouse and Ruby mouse, they came along to support me, but I think they've run off to find something sweet to eat."

Little Imogen, Charlie's sister, jumped up to Charlie and gave him a big hug and kiss and said, "Charlie, I've missed you so much, I love you. Are you coming home with us?"

"You bet I am, I can't wait."

"Come on then," said Imogen, "let's all go home."

"Just a minute, I need to thank my friends for helping me," said Charlie.

"Max, Ollie and Seb, thank you so much for helping me find my family, I couldn't have done it without you all and will you thank Ed for me and also tell Mouse that I'm sorry I disturbed him by shouting and jumping on his doll's house. Oh, and also tell him that I hope he will take Ruby home with him and live happily ever after."

"We will," said Max, "and don't go getting lost again, will you?"

"I won't, we're going to stick together from now on and no playing hide and seek." And with that, Charlie and his family thanked Max and his friends again and set off home, waving and shouting goodbye whilst Charlie started to tell his family the whole story of his getting lost, going through the door in the jungle and ending up in Nani's doll's house and their journey to find his family.

Book 8

Beware of the Mud

Max, Ollie and Seb breathed a sigh of relief and decided to find an empty table and have a rest and something to eat, so off they went to the nearest table where there was fruit, cakes and tea.

"I'm hungry," said Max. "Anyone for cake?" And they all nodded and helped themselves to everything that was spread before them and then washed it all down with a nice cup of tea.

They were all enjoying this nice rest and could see that the chimpanzees at the tea party were all packing up and making tracks back home.

Ollie said, "It's getting late and I think we need to be making tracks ourselves, it's a good way over Mumble Mountain and we need to get back before dark."

"Hang on a minute," said Max, jumping up from the table. "Has anyone seen Mouse and Ruby, the last I saw of them was when they both ran off to find morsels to eat at the tables?"

"Blimey," said Seb. "You're right, I haven't seen them either since they ran off together, I hope they are all right."

"We have to find them, I said I would take good care of Mouse and Ruby, too," said Max.

"That's going to be difficult, Mouse and Ruby are so teeny, tiny, where do we start?" asked Ollie.

"Right," said Max. "We'll do the same as we did before, we'll go in different directions, left, right and centre. Ollie you take left, Seb you go right and I'll look around the centre of the clearing."

"OK, let's go and look for something bright red with white spots."

So, they each went off in their allotted directions, peering closely on the ground in front of them, looking for Ruby in her bright red and white spotted dress, because if they could find Ruby, then surely Mouse wouldn't be far away from her and Max had already decided that when they found them, he would take Ruby back with Mouse to Nani's doll's house. That's if she wanted to come back with him.

Because Seb was slithering along the grass, he had a better chance than the others of seeing the mice and he kept a beady eye closer to the ground.

Max was on the middle path through the clearing and as he ran towards the edge of the jungle, he suddenly saw a flash of red and white spots running through the grass in front of him and heading towards the jungle.

"There's Ruby!" shouted Max to the others. "I can see her and Mouse must be with her. I'm on the middle path through the clearing heading for the jungle. Follow me."

Ollie spotted Max and shouted to Seb, "Come here, Seb. Wind yourself around my trunk, I'll give you a ride. We can move quicker to catch up with Max." Seb slithered quickly up to Ollie and wrapped himself around Ollie's trunk. With Seb securely entwined, Ollie took off, running as fast as he could in Max's direction.

Max could now see both Mouse and Ruby clearly, running together at full speed into the jungle. Mouse and Ruby, light as a feather, ran and ran across a muddy patch of land just on the edge of the jungle and Max followed as fast as he could.

Unbeknownst to him, this muddy patch of ground was quicksand. Mouse and Ruby were so tiny and light that they barely touched the surface of the quicksand as they ran, but Max being bigger and heavier soon began to sink into the mud as he ran into the middle of the patch. The quicksand began to devour him slowly, deeper and deeper, as it continued to pull him deeper into its depths.

"I'm sinking. I'm stuck!" shouted Max at the top of his voice. "Help, help, I'm stuck and can't get out!' Mouse and Ruby heard him shouting. They stopped in their tracks, turned and saw Max slowly sinking into the quicksand.

"Oh, Ruby," said Mouse. "Max is in trouble, how can we help him?"

"I don't think we can," replied Ruby. "We're not strong enough to pull him out. Where did Ollie and Seb go?"

"I don't know," said Mouse and they both just stood there, watching and realising they were about to lose their friend.

Just then, Ollie and Seb, still clinging to Ollie's trunk, came careering towards the patch of quicksand. They heard Max continually shouting, "Help, help, please help me!'

Ollie came to an ungainly halt at the edge of the mud and saw Max slowly being sucked under.

"What are we going to do?" asked Seb as he uncoiled himself and dropped to the ground.

"I don't know," answered Ollie. "I really don't know."

"Well, we'd better do something, or Max is going to be sucked below the surface of the quicksand and then he will be gone."

"I've got an idea," said Ollie.

"Well, come on, quick tell me what it is, we don't have much time."

"Right," ordered Ollie. "Seb, you wind yourself around the end of my trunk and hold on tight, then I'll walk to the very edge of the quicksand, you slither across the mud and grab hold of Max's arm and then I'll walk backwards. As I keep walking backwards, you'll be pulling Max out of the mud, keep holding him tight and I'll keep on pulling you both across the quicksand and out onto firm ground."

"That sounds like a plan," said Seb.

"We're coming to get you, Max!" shouted Ollie as Seb wound himself around the end of Ollie's trunk. Ollie walked as near to the edge of the quicksand as he could and Seb slithered head-first across the mud.

Seb shouted to Max, "I'm coming to get you, I'm nearly there. I'm going to wind myself around your arm, Max, so hold on tight, we'll get you out."

"Hurry, hurry!" shouted Max.

Seb reached for Max's arm and coiled his body around it and told Max to hold on tight. He then shouted to Ollie, "I've got him, pull, pull!'

Ollie started to back up steadily and as he did so, Seb and Max were being hauled out of the mud.

"Pull, pull!" shouted Max and Seb.

"I am pulling!" shouted Ollie. "I have to back up slowly so that you can both keep hold, trust me." Ollie continued to walk backwards, one step at a time, pulling Seb and Max out of the mud and back on to terra firma (firm ground).

Max was gasping for breath, shaking from head to toe with fear as he just lay on the ground in disbelief that he was still alive.

"Are you alright, Max?' asked Seb. Max raised himself and looked at Seb and Ollie and said, "Thank you for saving my life. I've been trying to look after Mouse and Ruby and I forgot I had to look out for myself, too."

"Don't mention it," said Ollie. "That's what friends are for. Come on, we need to get you all back home."

"Where are Mouse and Ruby?" asked Max.

"They're over there feeling sorry for themselves," said Ollie. "They know they shouldn't have run off from us, but I'm sure they've learned their lesson."

"And what lesson is that?" asked Seb.

"Not to think only of themselves but to think about others, too, like Max, you and I do," said Ollie.

"I'm sure they've learned that lesson. Haven't you, Mouse?" shouted Max.

"Yes, we have, Max." said Mouse. "Can I still come home with you to the doll's house?" asked Mouse. "And can Ruby come, too?"

"Sure, you can," said Max. "Come on, run around the outside of the area of quicksand and we can be on our way."

Mouse and Ruby ran as quickly as they could around the edge of the muddy area and came to a stop in front of Max.

"Okay," commanded Ollie. "Max, you put Mouse and Ruby in each of your pockets, then stand in front of me and climb up my trunk and onto my back.

Seb, you wrap yourself around my tail and we can set off back home to the doll's house."

Max, with Mouse and Ruby, carefully installed in his pockets, climbed up Ollie's trunk and sat himself down on Ollie's back whilst Seb wound himself around Ollie's tail and they all set off towards Mumble Mountain, the way home.

Book 9

Edward the Eagle to the Rescue

No word was said on the journey and it wasn't long before Ollie was winding his way up along the path to the top of Mumble Mountain. Max was safely seated on Ollie's back, Mouse and Ruby were snuggled in each of Max's pockets and Seb was clinging, quite uncomfortably to Ollie's tail. On reaching the top of the mountain, it started to blow up a bit of a gusty wind.

"Hold on tight," instructed Ollie. "It gets a bit breezy up at the top here."

"Okay!" shouted Max, as Mouse and Ruby popped their little heads out of his pockets to see what was going on. Mouse started to show off in front of Ruby by climbing up out of the pocket because he wanted to share the pocket that Ruby was in. At the same time, Ruby decided she wanted to share Mouse's pocket to keep warm and as both Mouse and Ruby jumped out of Max's pockets, a gust of wind lifted them both up into the air and blew them away.

"Mouse, Ruby!" shouted Max as the two mice were being blown away in the wind over Mumble Mountain.

"Ollie, Seb!" shouted Max. "Mouse and Ruby have been blown out of my pockets, stop, stop!" Ollie stopped in his tracks and they all looked up to see Mouse and Ruby being blown away by the wind.

As they watched, they saw something else soaring through the skies. "There's Ed the Eagle!" shouted Max. "What's he doing here? Ed, Ed!" shouted Max as loud as he could and what they all saw next was amazing. They saw Ed the eagle soaring through the sky and with his eagle eye, he spotted Mouse and Ruby being blown away. Ed picked up speed and flew

towards the two mice. Ed caught up with Mouse and Ruby and picked each one of them up with his claws, without hurting them, and flew them back to Max, Ollie and Seb and deposited them back into Max's pocket.

"Learn your lesson, mice, you could have been blown away and eaten by another eagle. Now stay in Max's pocket and don't move until you get home to the doll's house, do you hear me?" commanded Ed.

Mouse and Ruby were quaking in their boots, if they had any. "Okay, we will," they both answered.

"Where did you come from, Ed?' asked Max.

"I said that I would keep an eye on you all and it's a good job that I did. Now, mind you all keep safe on the way home," said Ed and with that, Ed flew off into the skies.

"Thank you, thank you," shouted Max.

"We need to get back to the doll's house. Come on, Ollie, let's go," said Max, to them all.

Ollie headed off again down the last leg of Mumble Mountain, back through the jungle towards the door to the cellar of the doll's house.

Book 10

The Doll's House

They were all tired on reaching the cellar door. Seb uncurled himself from Ollie's tail, Max climbed down Ollie's trunk, with Mouse and Ruby still safely in his pocket. "Thank you, Ollie and Seb," said Max. "Thank you for taking care of us all on this adventure."

"Thank you," said Mouse and Ruby. "We're sorry to have been such a pain. We won't be naughty anymore now that we're home."

"Well, that's good to hear," said Ollie. "You stay in Max's doll's house and you'll be safe enough there."

They were all about to say goodbye to one another when Max suddenly said, "Hold on a minute. How am I going to get into the doll's house, I'm too big?"

"Come on, Max, you should know how this works by now. Think yourself small," answered Mouse.

"Oh, I forgot," said Max. He closed his eyes, took a deep breath and thought himself small again. He felt a funny feeling all over his body and when he opened his eyes, sure enough, he was as small as Mouse and Ruby and was looking up now at Ollie and Seb, who seemed gigantic.

"Well, so long Ollie and Seb. Thank you for keeping us safe," said Max.

"Don't mention it," said Ollie. "It's been quite an adventure. It's been great to meet new friends and if you're ever in the jungle again, give us a shout. Bye, bye."

Max, Mouse and Ruby shouted and waved goodbye. "We'd better go into the doll's house, come on," said Max.

Max, Mouse and Ruby opened the door of the cellar to the doll's house and went inside and up the stairs. Max opened the front door of the house and jumped down into the bedroom. He closed his eyes, took a deep breath and thought himself big again and when he opened his eyes, he was back to his original size of a six-year-old little boy. He looked into the doll's house and saw Mouse and Ruby waving him goodbye. He waved back and said, "Good night, little mice, sweet dreams, don't let the bed bugs bite."

Book 11

Was It All a Dream?

In the morning, Nani shouted "Max, it's morning, time to get up, breakfast is ready."

Max opened his eyes and thought, *What a dream I've had. It was about Mouse and the doll's house. Mouse and I were in the jungle with a chimpanzee, an elephant, a snake and there was an eagle and oh, there was another mouse wearing a red and white polka-dot dress.*

"Coming now, Nani!" shouted Max.

Max got out of bed and opened the door of the doll's house and to his surprise, he saw a mouse in stripy pyjamas and a mouse in a red and white polka-dot dress, both tucked up in bed.

Maybe, it wasn't a dream after all, thought Max, as he ran downstairs for breakfast.

BY THE WAY, IT WASN'T A DREAM. NANI WROTE THE STORY OF MAX, MOUSE AND THE DOLL'S HOUSE, ESPECIALLY FOR ME. I JUST REMEMBERED IT IN MY DREAMS.